Tess Builds a Snowman

Homework

Write directions for something you know how to do, or write about something you know how to make.

It was snowing when Tess got home from school.
It snowed and snowed and snowed!
"I can make a snowman!" said Tess.

First, Tess rolled a big, big ball of snow.

Next, she rolled a smaller ball.
She plopped it on top of the big ball.

Then, Tess rolled the smallest ball for the head.
She put the balls together and patted them.

Last, she added a face, a scarf, and a hat.
"Now I have to do my homework," said Tess.

"And I know just what to do!"

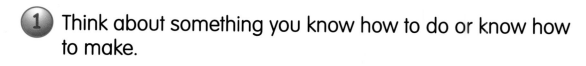

1. Think about something you know how to do or know how to make.

2. Write clear directions for your activity by using words like **first, next, then,** and **last**. Or you can make a numbered list of your directions.

3. Illustrate your directions.

First
Next
Then
Last

1.
2.
3.
4.